TOBY

the

Toothless Shark

A. W. LLEWELLYN HARVEY

Ordering Information:

For orders and inquiries, please contact:
1-888-404-1388
www.goldtouchpress.com
book.orders@goldtouchpress.com

Printed in the United States of America

Toby the Toothless Shark lived just outside of the Sea Kingdom of Paradise. Toby was a very large shark who loved to spend his days chasing the other fish in the neighbourhood. He was not very nice at all and made all the other fish in the Kingdom scared and unhappy. So much so that they hardly ventured out from the Kingdom and if they did had to make sure they were close to the rocks and small caves that Toby was too big to access. The Kingdom was their safe haven as Toby was not allowed in due to his nasty and aggressive nature. He just sneered at them as he passed by and opened his mouth to reveal a very large and very scary row of pointed jagged teeth. He just loved the effect he had on the other fish – it just made his day! Toby was a nasty bully.

Olivia Taylor

One day Toby woke up planning his usual pranks but somehow today he did not feel quite the same he had a nagging pain in his jaw and the more he tried to ignore it the worse it seemed to get – what was he going to do – this was certainly not going to be the fun day he had planned.

He circled round and round the outside of the Kingdom but his mind was not on the other fish just on this nagging deep pain in his jaw. He passed the entrance to the cave of Dr. Cowpolly twice before he remembered that Dr. Cowpolly was a dentist and maybe could help him with this pain.

DR. CONNOLLY
THE DENTIST

At the entrance he met with the Sergeant Majors who were Dr. Cowpolly's assistants he told them he would prefer to wait right there until Dr. Cowpolly could see him. By this time he was writhing about in pain and banging into things and the Sergeant Majors were nervous of the damage he could cause so made sure he got in to see Dr. Cowpolly right away as they just wanted to get rid of him as quickly as possible. The waiting room was full of waiting patients who were asked to return tomorrow and were quite happy to do so as they had grown very wary seeing the noise and disturbance that Toby was making.

Dr. Cowpolly did a quick inspection and immediately summoned Dick the Octopus into the room to wrap his tenticles around Toby's mouth to keep it open and Spiney the Lobster to clean them so Dr. Cowpolly could see more clearly.

Toby's tooth was in very bad shape and Dr. Cowpolly advised Toby that he would need an operation to extract it. Toby was in so much pain by this time that he just wanted it done and quickly and rudely told Dr. Cowpolly to "just get on with it".

Mr. Squidly and Mr. Moray were summoned into the operating room and Dr. Cowpolly numbed Toby's jaw with the ink from Mr. Squidly and Mr. Moray gently massaged Toby to quieten him down. A glint suddenly appeared in the corner of Dr. Cowpolly's eye and he almost broke into a grin as he began to make his plans.

BRUSH YOUR JAWS
FLORIDE
BIBS
TOOLS
TOOTHBRUSH
Olivia Taylor

As the pain became less and less from the triple dose of numbing ink and the massaging relaxed him Toby gradually fell into a deep sleep in the comfy dentist's chair while Dr. Cowpolly worked on and on and on - late into the day. This was the longest operation that Dick the Octopus ever remembered and he really hoped it would be over soon as his tentacles were getting very stiff and he was in an uncomfortable position behind Toby.

At last it was over and Dr. Cowpolly advised Dick to release Toby's jaw gently and allow him to sleep it off. Dr. Cowpolly looked well pleased and was mumbling to himself about justice being served and it was not until Dick looked into the large shell beside Toby's mouth did he realize what Dr. Cowpolly had done. He had removed not just one but ALL of Toby's teeth!

Olivia Taylor

Toby awoke feeling much better – thanked Dr. Cowpolly and swam away quickly to begin his usual round of fun chasing the other fish. He swam around and around opening his mouth to scare them all but something was different this time – they did not hide from him – they did not swim away as fast as they could – they seemed to be all whispering and laughing at him! He became more angry and aggressive but it did not seem to bother them. This was no fun at all so Toby swam home to practice his scary faces in the mirror and it was only then he realised he had no teeth!

Olivia Taylor

He was so angry he swam straight back to seek revenge on Dr. Cowpolly only to find that the cave was firmly guarded by Porcupine fish. He was about to attack regardless but his anger caused him to have such a headache that he decided to just swim away.

For the next few days he tried and tried to scare them all but no-one seemed frightened anymore and he was also finding it very difficult to capture and chew his food properly being hungry all the time made him even more grumpy. Without his daily fun of bullying he became very depressed and mopey. He had no friends to play with and was very lonely. He began to think that if he had not chased and frightened them maybe they would be his friends today and he would not be so miserable. A difficult lesson to learn. He also noticed that every time he got angry he also got a headache – that was not much fun either.

He now spent his days just floating around in the shallow water by the beach. He saw people each day and they seemed to be having fun with each other and he wanted to join in and have the same fun but when they saw him swimming about they rushed out of the water as quickly as they could. No-one wanted to be his friend and he became more and more unhappy. He took to keeping out of sight behind a big rock with a small pool and just lay there watching them having fun in the water and getting more and more depressed.

Olivia Taylor

Billy Jack and his parents were camping near the beach as they did every summer for the holidays. Billy Jack's mother had become very concerned when she saw Toby swimming in the water and would not allow Billy Jack to go in the water with his friends anymore as she told him it was too dangerous. Billy Jack now spent his days wandering along the shoreline and rocks just looking around to see what he could find. He found many different fish and sea creatures swimming in the small rock pools and each day he ventured further and further along the shoreline.

One day he turned a corner and came face to face with Toby in his shallow pool. Billy Jack was scared but Toby looked so lifeless just lying there without moving that Billy Jack took one step closer and then another and another until he was so close he could reach out and touch Toby. He could not stop himself and he reached out and touched him. Toby immediately reacted and opened his mouth and all Billy Jack could do was stare – he was not scary after all – he had no teeth!

Billy Jack spent the afternoon with Toby gently stroking him and cupping his hands to pour water over him – he didn't leave until late afternoon and ran all the way back to camp to tell his father. His father was initially shocked but Billy Jack begged him not to tell his mother at least until he had seen Toby so they set out the very next day to see if he was still there.

Toby was there and he was just as lifeless as before and opened his mouth to reveal no teeth and Billy Jack's father knew that he could not harm anyone but wondered why he was so listless with no interest in anything.

They took to visiting Toby every day and each day they noticed a little improvement Toby's eyes seemed to light up when he saw them.

Billy Jack wanted to swim with Toby and his father could not see a problem with that except they had to get Toby out of the rock pool. At high tide they gave him a tug and he swam out easily and both Billy Jack and Toby frolicked and played in the water. Toby felt happier than he had in months at last he had a friend.

One day Billy Jack had a thought - wouldn't it be fun to ride on Toby's back - and he ran back to his camp to fetch a piece of rope. Back at Toby's pool he attached the rope through Toby's mouth to use as a harness and he climbed on Toby and Toby gently swam out of the rock pool as Billy Jack guided him and swam around in the bay area for about twenty minutes before returning to the pool.

Olivia Taylor

Billy Jack dismounted and sat on the rocks looking at Toby - he was wondering if during their ride Toby was trying to tell him something as he had continually ducked under the water as if he wanted to go somewhere? He wished he could better understand Toby.

The next day Billy Jack took the harness and this time added his snorkel gear to his bag and ran off to visit Toby. Toby was waiting as usual and soon they were off around the bay. Toby began to dive and each time he went a little deeper and for a little longer seemingly to guage if Billy Jack was OK with this new venture. Billy Jack was thrilled and looking through his snorkel mask was truly amazed at what he saw. Sea plants — creatures and fish he had never seen before all living in perfect harmony and they seemed to come out to welcome Toby and his new friend — what a happy place Billy Jack thought.

Toby had been allowed back into the Kingdom once he had proved himself worthy and obeyed the two main rules. Mrs. Cowpolly had explained them to him – everyone swam very slowly in the kingdom and everyone was to be treated with respect and kindness.

One day as Toby was idling the time away munching on Sea Grass at the entrance to the Kingdom he looked up to see an old acquaintance Whitey the Great swimming into the Kingdom. He hadn't seen him in years since they swam the southern oceans together.

Whitey immediately recognised Toby and swam over to ask for his help. After the intital greetings he explained to Toby that he had been chasing Sea Lions and he crunched down on what he thought was a Sea Lion but turned out to be a floating log – he lost some teeth at the time and ever since then his jaws had been in great pain. Dr. Cowpolly had been recommended to him and he had travelled many miles - taking weeks to get here so he just needed directions to his office. Toby suddenly remembered how unpleasant Whitey had been to him at their last meeting when he suggested that Toby would probably end up as Shark Fin Soup as he could not swim as fast and was not as big as he was.

Toby was more than happy to oblige knowing full well Dr. Cowpolly's reputation for extraction rather than repair!

When they arrived Dr. Cowpolly was in the middle of removing a tooth from Goggles the Squirrel Snapper but Dr. Cowpolly assured them he would fit Whitey in as he had travelled so far to reach him and was in pain. As Dr. Cowpolly was working on Goggles a family of Mullets rushed into the office as if they were being chased.

The Sergeant Majors immediately surrounded the Mullets and as Dr. Cowpolly could not stop what he was doing Mrs. Cowpolly stepped in to scold them and remind them of the Kingdom rules of respect for others and to swim at a very slow pace. The Mullets apologised saying it was in their nature to swim fast and they just wanted to reach Dr. Cowpolly quickly but promised to never swim fast in the Kingdom again.

Beautiful Jaws
are
Created Here
Dr Conpolly's
DENTIST
Olivia Taylor

Dr. Cowpolly completed the extraction of Goggles and then explained to the Mullets that he could not attend to them now as he was very busy and he would stop by to see them tomorrow to arrange an appointment on his way to make a house call on Grandpa Rock – he arranged to visit him every six months for teeth cleaning and although Spiney the Lobster did all the work he just did the examination Grandpa Rock usually liked him to stay and talk and this usually ended up being the entire day but Dr. Cowpolly never minded as Grandpa Rock was so old and wise that he learned a lot from these conversations.

He sighed thinking to himself that this was going to be another very very long day and summoned his usual assistants to help prepare Whitey for surgery.

After the operation Whitey stayed with Toby to recuperate and learned how to change his diet after having his teeth removed. Toby told him the Sea Grasses were really not bad at all and that he felt much healthier with his new diet. Although Whitey was initially shocked and somewhat angry that all his teeth had been removed he was so glad to have no more pain and had seen how well Toby was coping that he decided just to relax and enjoy the kingdom.

When Whitey was strong enough to go for a swim Toby took him to his pool to wait for Billy Jack and introduce them.

Billy Jack arrived at the usual time for his swim and was really astonished to find Whitey in the rock pool and also a little wary due to his size. Toby nodded to Whitey to open his mouth to show Billy Jack that he had no teeth – so still a little hesitant Billy Jack reached out to touch Whitey and the touch then turned into a stroke and a pat and they both felt more comfortable with each other.

Billy Jack took to taking turns riding both Toby and Whitey and as the summer was coming to a close thought it may be fun to show his friends what he could do. He told them to keep it a secret and they were really excited to meet Toby and Whitey and even more excited when Billy Jack offered them a ride!

On the very last day of the holiday before they broke camp it was a tradition for all the campers to join together for a barbecue on the beach they built a fire from the driftwood to cook and sang songs well into the evening - it was always a good time. As a surprise this year the parents had arranged for a visit from the Ice Cream Truck.

Billy Jack thought it would be fun and also a bit mischievous to put all his friends on Whitey and he would lead on Toby and swim along the beach in front of all the parents – it would be a thrill and he just wanted to see the expression on their faces!

They swam along the beach on the back of Whitey and Toby and shouted out to their parents who reacted in horror but Billy Jack's father quickly assured them that it was fine and the two sharks were harmless and their look of fear changed to a look of amazement. What an incredible sight!

As soon as the children heard the bells of the Ice Cream truck arriving they jumped off Whitey and swam to the beach leaving Billy Jack to continue the ride with Toby and Whitey.

ICE-CREAM
POPSICLES
Olivia Taylor

Billy Jack went to see his friends in the kingdom for one last visit – he saw the Sergeant Majors – Dr. Mrs. Cowpolly – Mr. Mrs. Moray – The Mullet family – Grandpa Rock – Goggles the Squirrel Snapper – Mr. Squidly – Dick the Otopus and Spiney the Lobster to name a few. He could also not leave out Mr. Hamlet who everyone nicknamed Romeo as he was always surrounded by a group of fish just gazing into his beautiful dusky pink and green eyes and today was no different. He said good-bye to everyone and returned with Toby and Whitey to the rock pool.

Olivia Taylor

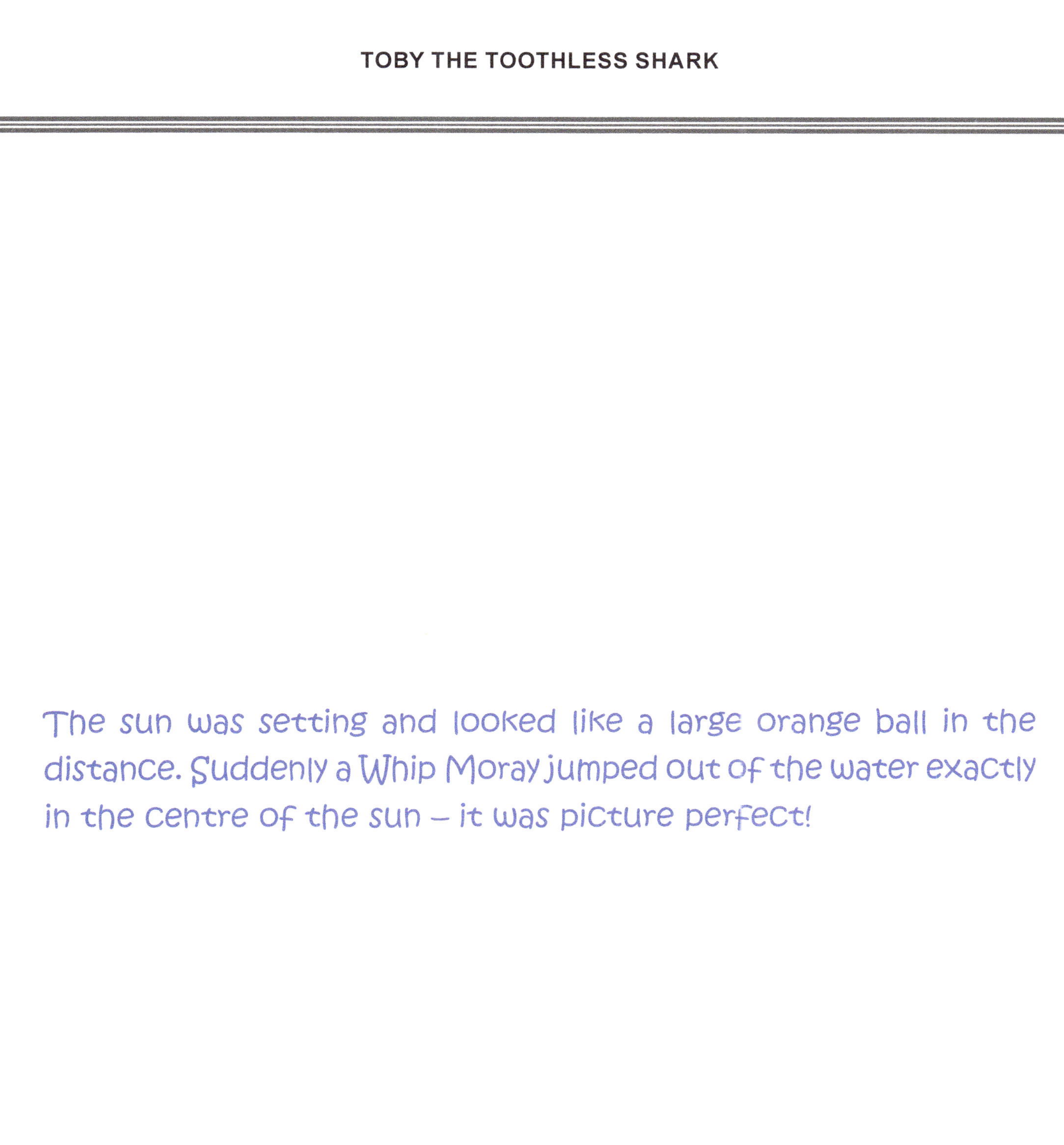

The sun was setting and looked like a large orange ball in the distance. Suddenly a Whip Moray jumped out of the water exactly in the centre of the sun – it was picture perfect!

Olivia Taylor

Billy Jack returned to the beach to have dinner, play and sing and of course Ice Cream! Then exhausted he went back to the camp to lie on his cot but for some reason he could not go to sleep thinking about Toby and how sad tomorrow would be leaving him. As he lay there looking up at the stars and searching for the small and big dipper he saw a shooting star followed by a fluorescent green trail – he made a wish that Toby and he would be friends for life and that Toby would wait for him until next summer. Feeling good that the wish would come true he fell into a sound sleep.

He awoke early next morning and rushed to Toby's pool to say good-bye but did not know how he could explain this to Toby so he just gave him a big hug and then picked up a sharp rock he had found and scored into the pool rock this message:-

"Goodbye Toby – see you next year - your friend forever Billy Jack"

Goodbye toby see you Next Ye
Olivia Taylor